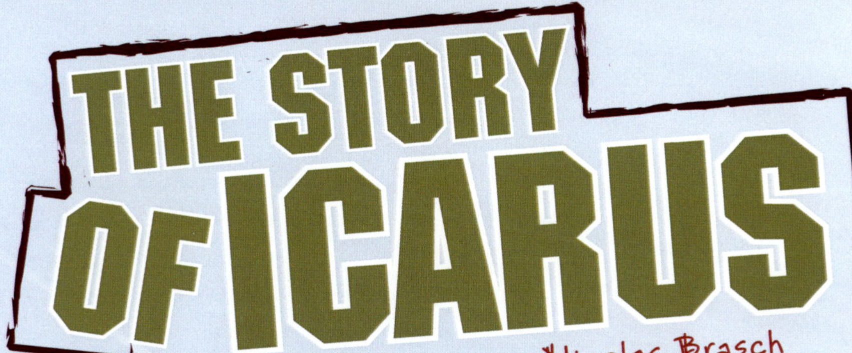
THE STORY
OF ICARUS
Nicolas Brasch
Alison Bride

The Story of Icarus

Text: Nicolas Brasch
Illustrations: Alison Bride
Editor: Rochelle Ransom
Design: Jennifer Warwick
Series design: James Lowe
Production controller: Lisa Porter
Reprint: Siew Han Ong

Fast Forward Independent Texts
Level 21

ISBN 978 0 17 017986 7
ISBN 978 0 17 017899 0 (set)

Cengage Learning Australia
Level 7, 80 Dorcas Street
South Melbourne, Victoria Australia 3205
Phone: 1300 790 853

Cengage Learning New Zealand
Unit 4B Rosedale Office Park
331 Rosedale Road, Albany, North Shore NZ 0632
Phone: 0508 635 766

For learning solutions, visit **cengage.com.au**

Printed in Australia by Ligare Pty Ltd
3 4 5 6 25 24 23 22

THE STORY OF ICARUS

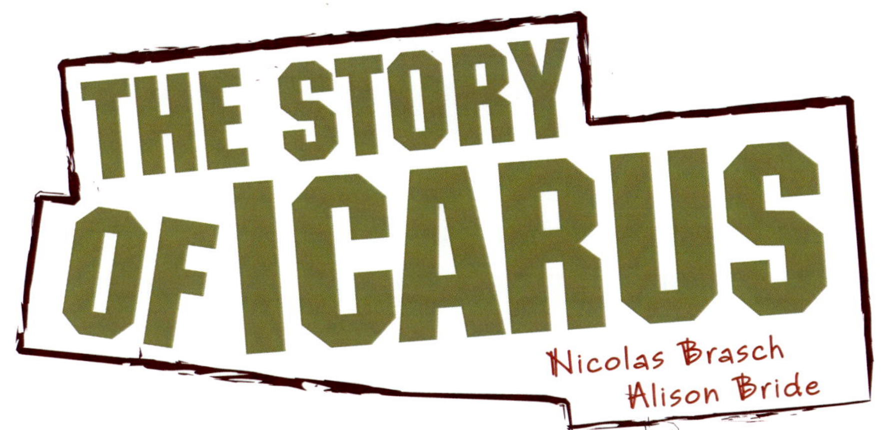

Nicolas Brasch
Alison Bride

Contents

The Labyrinth

Icarus was the son of Daedalus,
an inventor and builder of great talent.
Daedalus was so good
that word of his skills
reached King Minos of Crete.

The King had one great fear.
He feared that his enemies
would break into his palace
and steal his gold and treasures.

One day King Minos brought Daedalus
and Icarus before him.
He ordered them to design a prison
that the King's enemies could be locked in,
and be unable to escape from.

Daedalus and Icarus put their minds to work
and designed a building
unlike any other structure in the world.

The prison was built and called the Labyrinth.
The Labyrinth puzzled
anyone who entered it,
as it contained many passages,
rooms and openings.

It was a maze from which
most people could not escape.

At first, King Minos was grateful to Daedalus for solving his problem.

But soon King Minos started to hear whispers that Daedalus was secretly helping the King's enemies.

King Minos's happiness soon turned to anger. He decided to lock Daedalus and Icarus in a tower within the Labyrinth.

The King said he would never let Daedalus and Icarus leave the Labyrinth.

CHAPTER 2

The Island Prison

Daedalus was sure that he and Icarus
could find their way out
of the Labyrinth.
After all, they had designed it.
But first, they needed to get out of
the tower.

There were always two guards
at the tower door.
However, Daedalus knew
that the guards were not well paid
and would help them escape
for a few gold coins.

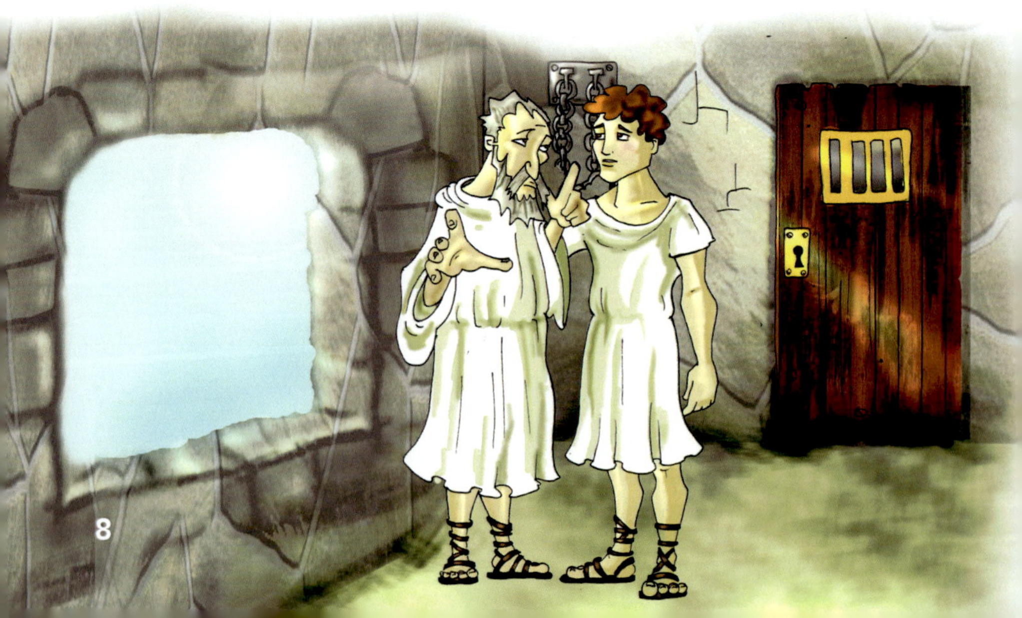

Daedalus told Icarus
that he was going to pay off the guards.

"Then," he continued,
"when they unlock the door and look away,
we will make our escape.
Just follow me and never lose sight of me –
not for one moment."

"But what happens
when we get out of the Labyrinth?"
asked Icarus.

Daedalus thought for a moment
and looked out of the window.

He had forgotten
that the tower was surrounded by sea.
The Labyrinth was, after all,
on an island.

"If we could get a boat..."
Daedalus thought to himself.
But then he remembered that King Minos
owned the fastest boats ever built.
Daedalus could never get a boat
that was faster than the King's.

"I fear we will be locked up forever,"
Daedalus said to his son, sadly.

He looked up at the sky.
Then he had an idea.

Feathers and Wax

Daedalus turned to Icarus.
"Maybe we could fly out of here," he said.

"Fly?" asked Icarus. "With what?"

Daedalus stopped and thought for a second.
Then he grinned from ear to ear.

Daedalus opened up his closed fist,
showing Icarus the shiny gold coins
in the palm of his hand.

"With this," he said.

Daedalus knocked on the door
to attract the guards' attention.

Icarus watched his father
speak with the guards.
Then Daedalus handed the coins
to the two men,
who accepted the payment greedily.

Early the next morning,
the guards entered the room.
One of them brought in some breakfast,
while the other dropped
four packages on the floor.

Daedalus quickly opened them.
One package contained feathers;
another had reeds;
the third package held wax;
and the fourth contained string.

Daedalus and Icarus got straight to work. They attached the feathers to the reeds with wax and string.

When they had finished, they held up their creations: four wings, two each.

Up, Up and Away

Daedalus and Icarus
stood at the window
and fitted the wings to their arms.

"Before we set off,"
Daedalus said to his son,
"I want you to promise me one thing."

"What?" asked Icarus.

"Do not fly too high,
lest the heat
from the sun
melts the wax
on your wings."

"I understand, Father,"
said Icarus.

"Just follow me," said Daedalus,
"and we will fly off the island,
across the sea,
safely to land."

"Are you ready?" Daedalus asked.

Icarus nodded,
although he was worried.

"Then let's fly," said Daedalus.

He leapt from the window ledge
and began flapping his wings.

Daedalus flew like a bird.

Then Icarus leapt from the window,
as his father had done.
He flapped his wings
and he too flew like a bird.
It was the most wonderful feeling
that Icarus had ever known.

Icarus flapped his wings
as hard as he could.
He climbed higher and higher.

He remembered what his father had told him,
but the feeling of flying was just too good.

So he kept flapping his wings
and continued to fly higher and higher.

CHAPTER 5

Tragedy Strikes

Daedalus soon looked behind him
and gasped in shock.
He could hardly see Icarus anymore.

Daedalus screamed out,
but Icarus was much too far away
to hear him.

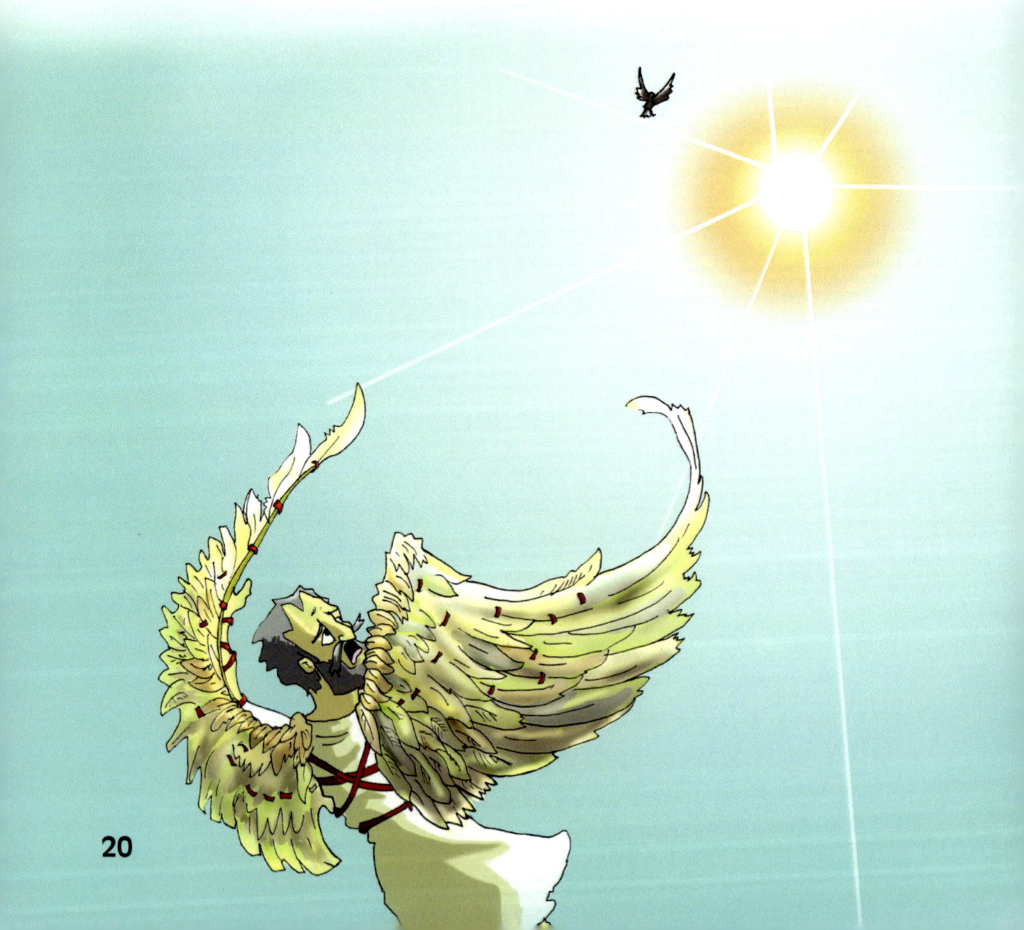

Icarus felt as if he ruled the world.

But this feeling did not last for long.
Soon, the heat from the sun
started melting the wax.
One by one,
the feathers began to drop off his wings.
Icarus started falling towards the sea.

Icarus flapped harder and harder,
without success.
The wax kept melting.
The feathers kept dropping.
Icarus kept falling.

In the distance,
Daedalus saw his son fall towards the sea.
As he watched, his heart broke.

Suddenly, Icarus was no longer in sight.

Daedalus flew towards
where he had last seen Icarus.
He looked down.

All he saw were feathers
floating on the water.
Daedalus screamed and cried,
for Icarus was gone.